SPORTS SUCCESS
Winning Women
in Ice Hockey

Marlene Targ Brill

BARRON'S

All inquiries should be addressed to:
Barron's Educational Series, Inc.
250 Wireless Boulevard
Hauppauge, NY 11788
http://www.barronseduc.com

Library of Congress Catalog Card No.: 99-24682
International Standard Book No.: 0-7641-1115-9

Library of Congress Cataloging-in-Publication Data
Brill, Marlene Targ.
    Winning women in ice hockey / by Marlene Targ Brill.
            p.   cm — (Sport success)
    Summary: An overview of the history of women's ice hockey, including how the game is played, equipment used, and biographies of four women players.
    ISBN 0-7641-1115-9
    1. Hockey for women Juvenile literature 2. Hockey players
Biography Juvenile literature. 3. Women hockey players
Biography Juvenile literature. [1. Hockey for women.
2. Hockey players. 3. Women Biography.] I. Title.
II. Series: Brill, Marlene Targ. Sport success.
GV848.6.W65B75   1999
796.962'082'092273—dc21   99-24682
                                                                        CIP

PRINTED IN THE UNITED STATES OF AMERICA
9 8 7 6 5 4 3 2 1

Contents

Acknowledgments

A hearty thank you to all those who generously gave their time and shared information. Without you, this book could never have been written. A round of applause for Wade Arnott, agent; Steve Bartlett, agent; Chris Callanan, agent; Wally Cozack, Olympic Oval senior coach; Danielle Defoe, Canadian Hockey Association; Mark Dunn, agent; Patty Hughes, USA Hockey Association; Marty Kirsch, teacher; Candy Knippenberg, teacher; John Marchetti, Yale coach; Mary Masters, Big Ten Conference; Robin Medintz, physical education teacher; Don Miller, high school coach; Marylin Wickenheiser, teacher; Peter Whitten, health center director.

A special thank you goes to the wonderful athletes who agreed to be interviewed for this book: Cammi Granato, Manon Rheaume, Erin Whitten, and Hayley Wickenheiser. Their commitment has made ice hockey possible for millions of girls everywhere.

A Note to Readers

Once upon a time there were girls who loved to run, shoot baskets, speed skate, race bicycles and cars, and climb to great heights. These girls were different from active females today. Instead of being applauded for their talents, they were told they *couldn't* and *shouldn't* play most sports.

As recently as the late 1800s, adults offered a host of reasons why girls should stick to their dolls and needlework. One reason followed the belief that exercise hurt the frail female body and tired the mind. Some doctors assumed that riding caused "bicycle face," a scrunched-up look that supposedly came from the strain of sitting forward on a bicycle seat. Most likely, the tight corsets, high collars, and big hats of the day led to the frowns.

Another common myth suggested that females who played like boys had something wrong with them. For one thing, active girls *looked* unladylike. Baron Pierre de Coubertin, founder of the modern Olympics, wrote in 1896: "It is indecent that spectators should be exposed to the risk of a woman being smashed before their very eyes."

Other critics assumed that females could never be as good in sports as males anyway. Therefore, they wondered, why would girls even bother to try? Such faultfinders called girls who played sports tomboys just because they wanted to have the same fun as boys.

Similar negative views of women in sports lingered into the 1960s. By then, females had started pushing for equal rights at home and at work. This led to Americans accepting that women and girls performed well in specific sports, such as gymnastics and figure skating.

Then the United States Congress passed the important Title IX law in 1972. Title IX ordered schools to give girls the same opportunities as boys to participate in sports. This meant that teams, equipment, and *all* sports had to be open to girls. Not long after the United States ruling, Canada and Australia passed similar laws. Each country required their schools to budget equal money for boys' and girls' sports. These laws championed the wild notion that girls would succeed if given the chance.

Little by little, schools began programming certain sports for girls. Some girls joined all-boy teams. Others battled to organize teams and leagues of their own. Gradually, females broke down barriers in sports such as sailboat racing, mountain climbing, wheelchair racing, coaching, and snowboarding that were mostly male-only arenas. Athletic girls who were once told to watch or cheerlead could now win their own medals.

At the same time girls entered more sports, new research replaced old-fashioned thinking that had kept girls on the sidelines. The Institute for Athletics and Education and the President's Council on Physical Fitness discovered that active girls earned better grades and were three times more likely to graduate from high school than their less active sisters. Girls who played sports were also more likely to go on to college and remain healthier as adults, developing fewer health problems such as heart disease. In 1999, the Big Ten College Conference reported that a record 80 percent of women leaders in the top 500 U.S. companies participated in sports. These figures showed that girls who played sports felt better about themselves. They developed more confidence all-around because sports taught them what it means to be strong in body and mind.

Updated studies plus Title IX have had an amazing impact on girls participating in sports. In 1972, only 1 of every 27 girls joined high school varsity sports. Today, 1 in 3 girls participate, reflecting a positive trend in women's athletics. Now more girls play soccer than the number of girls who joined all sports in 1970. Consider, too, that in 1972, only 96 women athletes from the United States competed in the summer Olympics. By the summer of 1996, the roster had climbed to 280 women.

The 1996 and 1998 U.S. Women Olympic winners for soccer, baseball, basketball, and ice hockey—all new Olympic sports—were loaded with players who got their start on high school and college teams because of Title IX. These players confirm the success of 20 years of giving girls the opportunity to strut their sport's stuff. Now that's progress!

Still, we have a long way to go toward equality for women in sports. One group to win over is the media. Except for sports such as ice skating, tennis, gymnastics, and now basketball, women athletes are invisible in most newspapers, television stations, and books. Donna Lopiano, former director of the Women's Sports Foundation, reported, "Until the 1990s, sports pages devoted more column inches to horses and dogs than to women's sports."

A 1990 study by the Los Angeles Amateur Athletic Foundation confirmed Ms. Lopiano's findings. The foundation tracked sports news in four major U.S. daily papers for three months. They discovered that men's sports received 81 percent of the coverage, women's sports obtained 3.5 percent, and neutral topics, such as Olympic sites, received 15.5 percent coverage.

Little has changed going into the twenty-first century. The joys and talents of women athletes in nontraditional sports have gone unsung for too long. This book series seeks to broadcast the news that active girls and women are involved in all sports. So, find the sport in this series that interests you most. Learn how other athletes have succeeded, often bucking great odds. Read how these talented women have fought battles so you can play any sport you choose. Then go out and play! Join the winning women and girls everywhere who are just warming up for a future of SPORT SUCCESS.

Marlene Targ Brill

Chapter One

On Your Mark,
Get Set . . .

ce hockey is an old European sport. Men played different forms of the game in Great Britain and France as far back as the sixteenth century. A wintry day turned an icy field into a great place to smack a brass ball around with a wooden club. By the middle 1800s, the Dutch strapped metal blades onto their shoes, replacing earlier blades of wood or bone. These new skates served as the forerunners of current ice skates. They added to a game that ushered in modern ice hockey.

Ice Hockey Comes to America

About the same time, North Americans learned about hockey from the British troops on duty in Canada. Bored soldiers passed the time by hitting a ball along frozen Canadian fields. Few set rules existed in the 1800s; players simply made them up as the need arose.

In 1867, soldiers prepared a field in Kingston, Ontario, for another version of ice hockey, this time with goalposts. The game marked the first recorded event in North American hockey history. Years later, hockey fans believed it was only fitting that Kingston be the site of hockey's first Hall of Fame.

By 1893, hockey had grown so popular that Lord Stanley, Canada's governor-general, donated a silver bowl to honor Canada's top team. This prize became known as the Stanley Cup, and the gift fueled Canada's hockey fever. Soon sports-minded men competed for the honor of winning the Stanley Cup, a trophy sought by top North American men's teams to this day.

Interest in ice hockey spread quickly throughout Canada and into the United States. Canada formed the first league of teams, the Amateur Hockey Association, in 1889. By 1910, an expanded league, the National Hockey Association, had started with teams from the United States as well. This organization grew into the National Hockey League (NHL) in 1917, the beginning of American men's professional hockey as we know it today. In 1924, men's ice hockey joined the Olympics, making it a recognized world-class game. Hockey for women was not far behind.

Women Take to the Ice

American women wanted to play hockey, too. But customs of the day limited what women could do, especially in sports. Although girls ice skated in the late 1800s, hockey was thought unladylike. Still, active women persisted in playing. Only players in the earliest games had to hide indoors and away from the gaping eyes of men.

Lord Stanley and his hockey-loving family gave women the chance to play in public. Lord Stanley liked the game so much that he built a rink at the Government House in Ottawa, Canada. Each day, his staff hosed the large lawn until it was a smooth sheet of ice. Then, the entire Stanley clan, Lord *and* Lady Stanley and their eight sons and two daughters, whizzed around the outdoor rink. The family was even seen skimming the ice on the Sabbath, a sin in Victorian times for sure!

An 1889 snapshot of daughter Isobel in a long skirt with a short hockey stick captures one of the first images of a woman playing hockey. The following year, a photographer shot the earliest known picture of women playing in an ice hockey game. From then on, women took to the ice in larger numbers, especially in Canada. Yukon gold miners built large indoor rinks in teeming mining towns. Universities and larger towns constructed arenas. Everywhere men played hockey, women demanded ice time, too.

Females usually received much less time on the ice, despite their complaints. Nevertheless, they managed to form hockey teams of their own as long as they dressed properly and played away from men. Women skated in layers of petticoats under heavy ankle-length skirts. Players swung sticks in long-sleeve blouses buttoned to the chin, the outfit of the day.

Some women used these overstuffed skirts to their advantage. They weighted the hems on the long, flowing skirts with buckshot. This kept skirts spread wider across the ice, blocking the other team's puck.

For years, women played their games mostly behind closed doors. When women's college teams competed, no male students were allowed to cheer them on. At McGill University in Montreal, women received ice time only if men were on duty to guard the entrances and players followed the rules to dress warmly. They competed in long linen skirts and snug **bulky** sweaters with emblems or letters to identify

Trophy-winning Queen's University team bundled from neck to toe in their toasty uniforms.

their team. These women never competed for famous prizes like the Stanley Cup. They seemed content to play hockey for the joy of the game.

A few university women bucked the rules. At Canada's Queen's College, the women's team challenged the men's team to a game. Their gutsy dare brought instant attack from university leaders who thought playing with men was an outrage. The women refused to back down. Instead, they charged fees for the public to watch their games. They called themselves the Love-Me-Littles because of the disapproval they received from the university. Yet, they filled the rink with audiences who loved to watch their lively stickhandling and swift passing and scoring.

Women's hockey teams from the United States and Canada began competing in 1916. From the start, people worried that hockey was too rough for girls. Another unproven fear was that females suffered more injuries. Hockey leagues argued that higher injury rates cost more to keep girls playing. But ice

RINGETTE

Between the 1960s and 1980s, the game of ringette gained popularity with hockey-loving girls. Some say that Ontario's Sam Jack invented the game to keep girls from playing the rowdier game of ice hockey. Ice hockey and ringette had similar rules. The main difference was that ringette allowed no body contact. Parents liked the idea of a safer "girls' game." And boys liked the idea of girls playing on their own teams.

With ringette, girls skated with sticks, as in hockey. Only rubber rings replaced pucks, and the sticks were straight. Stickhandling involved scooting the ring into the net with the stick's point inside its circle.

Today, ringette has been adapted for school gym classes and inline games. The sport has fans in the United States, Europe, Japan, and Russia. Some women's hockey pros never knew they could play anything but ringette as youngsters. Canadian Olympic forward Judy Diduck played ringette from age ten until 1990. That year, she ended her ringette career to join the national ice hockey team at age twenty. And she hasn't stopped playing ice hockey since.

hockey was a dangerous sport for boys, too. In the early days of American hockey, no one wore padded gear or face masks. Small wonder that there were so many injuries!

In 1927, Queen's goaltender Elizabeth Graham played a historic game bedecked in a wire fencing mask to guard her face. Her bold invention didn't catch on until 1959. That's when Montreal's Jacques Plante set a new goalie trend for males by wearing a mask for each game he played. Still, protective gear for women was a long way off. Money was short, and the only available equipment for girls, if there was any, belonged to the boys' teams. Never mind that girls were built differently from boys.

Until the middle 1900s, men's groups controlled most women's hockey. Canadians were the first to form the Ladies Ontario Hockey Association in 1930, which gave women the right to make decisions about their games. In the United States, female athletes continued to play under male supervision. A U.S. Athletic Union manager claimed that "there has been no demand for a separate federation. The women prefer to remain under masculine rule."

Women Soccer Players Have Their Say

In fact, restless women on both sides of the border tired of men telling them what to wear and how to play. But it took another thirty years for women to receive enough international attention to strengthen their voice and gain important ice time. In 1967,

Canada's Dominion Ladies Hockey Association hosted its first women's world tournament in Brampton, Ontario. It was the largest women's tournament of the day.

By 1970, women's hockey teams had formed in Sweden, Finland, Japan, China, Korea, Norway, Germany, and Switzerland. Teams representing Canadian provinces and colleges mushroomed. The United States saw a similar increase in college and club teams for girls.

As the 1970s unfolded, women's hockey changed dramatically with movements for women's equality and Title IX. The National College Athletic Association (NCAA) finally recognized women's ice hockey in the United States. Its Eastern College Athletic Conference (ECAC) sponsored two new leagues for university women.

Tournaments now attracted more teams and larger crowds. Fans enjoyed the skillful sport that females played without the usual body bashing of men's hockey. Girls received proper training and, for the first time, special chest pads and pelvic guards designed just for them. Parents saw how safe hockey could be when played with the right uniforms and practice.

Women's Ice Hockey Today

The biggest boost for modern women's hockey came in 1987. Canada hosted the first Women's World Invitational tournament with teams from the United

States, Sweden, Switzerland, Holland, and Japan. The spirit of women's hockey was so strong at the games that the International Ice Hockey Federation decided to create the Women's World Championship in 1990. From then on, the world community of women's hockey players gathered every two years to compete. Now, devoted young players could dream of hockey beyond their childhood rink.

Women hockey players finally achieved recognition for their sport, but this wasn't enough. For these athletes, full acceptance meant a chance to play in the Olympics. Die-hard players also wanted a professional league so they could earn a living as men did playing the game they loved.

A chance at the Olympics came after the second Women's World Championship in 1992. Officials of the International Olympic Committee couldn't help but notice the high quality of play among participants. After much prodding, officials agreed to include women's ice hockey as a full medal sport beginning in 2002. Japan decided to invite women's hockey to their 1998 Olympic games four years earlier than required. A new day was dawning for women's hockey.

The greatest tribute to women's hockey came in 1998. Sixty-four years after men's hockey joined the Olympics, women took to the Olympic ice in Nagano, Japan. In the final game, the United States topped Canada's team by winning the gold over Canada's silver medal. Just after the Olympics, female hockey stars began receiving celebrity status usually reserved for men. Their faces adorned cereal boxes, television advertisements, and magazine ads. Finally, women earned the money and recognition to play hockey.

Since the world competition, the number of females playing ice hockey has skyrocketed. Between 1990 and 1997, the rate multiplied fourfold. Most girls joined mixed teams of boys and girls. Many others played on newly created female leagues. Whereas 149 U.S. girls' and women's teams skated in 1990, almost 910 teams competed by 1997, with the promise of many more.

Minnesota led the way. In 1993, the Minnesota State High School League mailed surveys to discover which sports females found most interesting. More than 8,000 girls chose ice hockey. The following spring, the league identified girls' ice hockey as a varsity sport. That meant that schools could send teams to represent them in tournaments with other school teams from the state. In the opening season, 24 schools joined. Apple Valley won the first Minnesota girls' state high school championship, the first in the country. By the 1997–98 season, 83 teams competed for the honor, and many other states had organized their own leagues. Countless local championships gave girls a turn to have fun while perfecting their skills for a chance at international fame.

Still, the greatest challenges are yet to come. Since 1998, world championships have become a yearly event. And, plans are in the works for the first women's professional league in the United States and Canada. By 2002, these teams will let girls everywhere know women can and do play ice hockey.

U.S. forward and team captain Cammi Granato celebrates winning the gold.

ABBY HOFFMAN CUP

In 1956, nine-year-old Abigail (Abby) became one of her league's top defense players. By the end of the season, she had made the Toronto league all-star team. That's when Abby's hockey headaches began.

She showed her birth certificate, as she had done to get on the first team. This time, however, officials noticed that their star player was a girl. After an uproar, they let her finish the season but kicked her out of the boys' league. Abby played in the few games offered for girls and then quit hockey. But the experience taught Abby an important lesson. Girls lacked the same basic rights to play sports that boys took for granted.

A talented athlete, Abby switched to track. She became a four-time Olympic athlete. Twice she reached the 800-meter (0.5-mile) finals; she won the gold in 1963. Yet, Abby still faced people who said running more than 800 meters could be harmful to females. This was at a time when she ran 56 kilometers (35 miles) a week to train.

Facing such unfairness, Abby began speaking out for athletes' rights. Her strong voice urged the sports community to give girls and women full and fair access to sports. In 1982, she helped found the Canadian Amateur Hockey Association's first national championships. For her role in supporting girls in sports, the championship's top prize was named the Abby Hoffman Cup.

Chapter Two

How to Play

ce hockey is a fast-paced game. Players need to skate quickly, control a stick for straight passes, and shoot hard. This is no game for gentle souls. Heather Linstad, Northeastern College coach, summed up the game in a *Chicago Tribune* article: "It's fast, it's fun, and it's competitive."

The Team

Ice hockey begins with two teams on a hockey field of ice. Their main job is to hit a *puck*, the flat hard rubber disk, into the other team's net. Each time the puck enters a net, the shooting team scores one point, or a *goal*. As with many team sports, the side with the most points wins.

Hockey is played on a large ice rink that is about 200 feet (61 meters) long and 85 feet (26 meters) wide. Five lines and five circles are painted on the ice. Six players from each team skate on the ice at one time, although teams involve up to 18 players total. Players have different jobs that depend upon where the coach positions them in the patterned rink.

Two blue lines separate the rink into three zones. Two players closest to their own goal net guard the *defensive zone. Defense people* protect the net by blocking the other team from getting near enough to score.

The opposite end from a team's net is called the *offensive zone.* This is where three *forwards* and a *center* dart and zigzag, trying to get free of the other

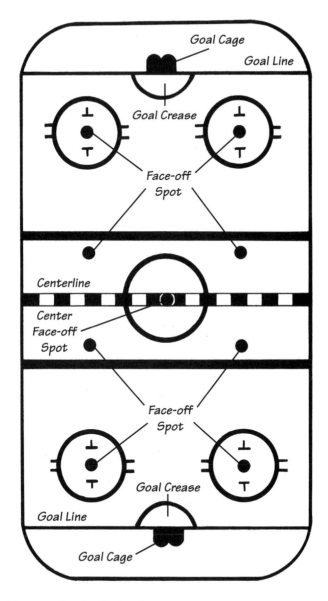

Markings on the ice for hockey.

team. They weave in and out for a clear shot into the other team's net.

A center also *faces off* with the center from the other team. This is done in one of the five circles drawn on the ice. During face-offs, the referee drops the puck between a center from each team. The centers scramble to gain control of the puck and shoot it to teammates. Face-offs begin sessions of play:

- at the start of the period
- after a goal is scored
- after a penalty or a time-out

Meanwhile, a thickly padded *goalie* protects each goal net at all times. This soldier guards the team's sacred kingdom from being invaded by the enemy's puck.

A game runs for three *periods*. Every period extends no longer than 20 minutes. In games with younger players, however, periods usually last 10 or 15 minutes. Each team is allowed to call one time-out during the game.

Equipment

Girls must be very strong for hockey. Hockey players wear many pounds of equipment. They pile and strip layers of special clothes and skates on and off before and after games. They lug their bundles to and from games. All this equipment is necessary to protect them while playing one of the most active team sports.

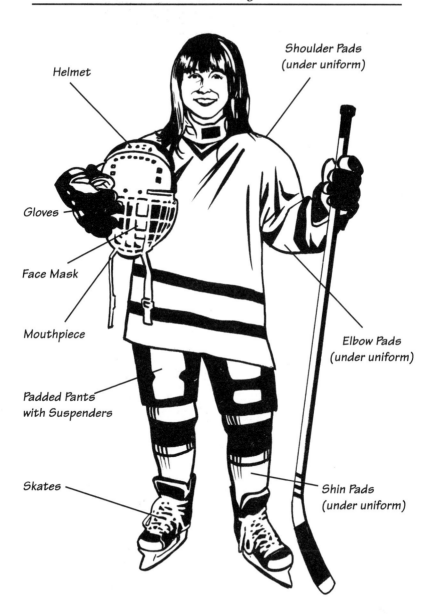

Helmet

Shoulder Pads
(under uniform)

Gloves

Face Mask

Mouthpiece

Padded Pants
with Suspenders

Skates

Elbow Pads
(under uniform)

Shin Pads
(under uniform)

Now special equipment is designed for a girl's body.

According to USA Hockey, the main professional hockey group, uniforms for girls include:

- an approved helmet with a face mask and a mouthpiece
- shoulder pads under the uniform
- elbow pads
- gloves
- padded pants with suspenders
- hockey skates
- specially made female shoulder/chest pads
- pelvic protectors

STICKS AND PUCKS

Sticks need as careful fitting as skates. A good length for most young players extends from the skated player's chin to the ice. Sticks can never measure more than 60 inches (152 cm). Most hockey sticks are made of ash wood inside a fiberglass covering. Blades, which are 12 1/2 inches (32 cm) long and 3 inches (7.6 cm) wide, gently curve to help guide the puck. Goalies and players have different sticks. Because a goalie's job is to stop the puck, her stick has a bigger blade. Players have thinner sticks with smaller blades to better steer and shoot the puck.

Pucks are usually made of hard rubber. Rules call for pucks that are 1 by 3 inches (2.5 by 7.6 cm) in diameter and between 5.5 and 6 ounces (155 and 170 grams). Several pucks are frozen before each game. Freezing helps them glide, rather than bounce, along the ice during play.

Goalkeepers need extra equipment to pad them against fast-flying pucks. Besides regular hockey gear, goalies wear an oversized catching glove, a shield-like blocker, higher leg pads, and chest padding.

Upper Body
Protector
(under uniform)

Blocker

Goal Stick

Leg Pads

Catching Glove

Padded uniforms protect goalkeepers from injury.

Team centers face off at the referee's signal.

REFEREES

Most formal games require three judges, or referees. Their jobs are to score goals and call time, penalties, and other game plays. Each referee wears a whistle, which is blown to stop the game clock whenever one of these calls occurs.

Girls' and Boys' Hockey

How is girls' ice hockey different from the boys' game? Generally, the play and equipment is similar. Still, there are differences.

Some say it's the rules. With girls' rules, no body checking is allowed—players cannot hit their opponents with hips or shoulders when trying to steal the puck. Without body checking, the game relies more on stickhandling than force to score. Yale University women's hockey coach John Marchetti says, "In the women's game, the fundamentals are easier to recognize. Moving the puck, making the extra pass, and playmaking are stressed."

For others who follow both games, the difference lies in the basic fact that preteen girls tend to develop differently from boys. Girls gain more body fat and grow up shorter than boys. This gives girls more energy for sports that require stamina, such as long-distance running. Growing boys, on the other hand, add more muscle and height than girls.

Before puberty, boys and girls can easily compete in the same leagues. As boys grow stronger and taller, however, their body build and size gives them an edge. This doesn't mean girls cannot play the same games as boys. Girls just need to understand that there may come a time when it's safer to join an all-female league.

Some differences between girls' and boys' games depend upon the general style of play. According to Heather Linstad, "The women's game is more deliberate in setting up plays, and much less physical. There is a penalty for checking, skating into someone. Instead of checking, (women) skate an opponent off the puck, like brushing someone aside.

"Our equipment is pretty much the same, but our pads are lighter. And we don't break nearly as many sticks as the men do. So our costs are less."

Those in the know, however, credit the spirit of female hockey players as making the biggest difference between genders. "There is a good deal less contention (conflict)," said John Marchetti. "The women . . . are much more into the team concept."

Perhaps this team spirit comes from years of suffering for the right to play. As adult players, these women are thrilled for the chance to enjoy themselves on the ice. These are the real hockey heroes, the women who battled great odds to play a game they were told they couldn't play. They struggled with angry communities, mean opponents, and the price of being "the only girl." These are the hockey players who opened doors for future generations of girls.

Here are some of their stories.

Chapter Three

Cammi Granato

Cammi Granato is one of the most visible U.S. women's hockey players. As forward, she zigzags across the ice, always appearing where the action is. Her sharp eye tracks the puck for a chance to score a goal. Careful stickhandling and a strong will to win have created one of the top scorers in women's hockey.

Cammi has been outscoring opponents most of her life, helping to thrust women's hockey further into the limelight. This six-time member of the U.S. Women's National Team is one of three players who has been with the program since it began. Her friendly, yet determined personality made her the perfect choice as captain of the first U.S. women's Olympic team, the winning players who brought home the gold in 1998.

Born to Skate

Cammi was born on March 25, 1971 in Maywood, Illinois. She grew up in a close-knit, supportive family. Cammi was second youngest of four boys and two girls. Her father, Don Granato, supervised his father's beverage business while her mother, Natalie, managed the busy household.

Neighbors knew the Granatos as a hockey family. Cammi's parents went on their first date to a Chicago Blackhawks game, and her father played amateur hockey. After the children arrived, family members took turns sharing season tickets to

Blackhawks' games. Cammi's brothers often kept out of trouble by knocking around a puck.

"Hockey was always part of my family," Cammi explained. "When I was five, my mom wanted me to figure skate. But when she took me to lessons, I skipped out to watch hockey. I told her 'I want to do that, too.' "

Cammi hit the ice before entering kindergarten, and she hasn't stopped skating since. One of her earliest fond memories involves learning to stop and start on skates, important skills for the game. Back then, her rink was a big frozen field across the street from the Granato's Broadview, Illinois home. When brothers Tony, Donny, and Robby headed for the outfield, Cammi tagged along, practicing her slap shots with the boys.

Then the family moved to nearby Downers Grove, leaving the makeshift rink too far away. Determined to play, Cammi and her brothers converted the basement into a hockey rink. They found little sticks and two nets and taped lines on the floor. Cammi's brothers and cousins fired rapid pucks at her, never giving her slack for being the youngest or a girl. She usually received the lion's share of pushes and shoves on

"When I was five, my mom wanted me to figure skate. But when she took me to lessons, I skipped out to watch hockey. I told her 'I want to do that, too.' "

the way to the net. The play was rough, but Cammi loved it.

"Those games got pretty intense," Tony told *American Hockey Magazine*. "But Cammi hung right in there, and she never backed down. She was one of the most . . . (dogged) kids I've ever seen."

Team Play

By age six, Cammi wanted to join a team but couldn't find girls her age who played. So she signed up with a brother and a cousin on the Downers Grove Huskies, a boys' team with the neighborhood youth program. Cammi remained the only girl in the league into her teens.

"When I was younger, being the only girl was no problem. The main difference was the rink only had a boy's locker room, so I changed in the bathroom. My teammates accepted me, and other boys had no idea to be prejudiced. One father didn't want his son playing on a team with a girl. Into the season, he apologized after he saw how I set up his son for goals," Cammi recalled.

By the time she was ten, however, many parents had changed their kids' thinking about girls in hockey. Occasionally, Cammi had to call herself Carl to qualify for a tournament. When she played as a girl, boys from different leagues gave her a hard time. Some couldn't wait to body check her. One coach threatened to have his boys "separate her shoulders" if she played in the game. Cammi's coach asked if she wanted to sit out, but she declared "no way." Cammi discouraged the bullies by outskating and outscoring them.

"Another time my cousin and I switched jerseys because we heard that the other team wanted to take me out the first time on the ice." Instead of being negative, Cammi shrugged off the threat. "We joked about it. My teammates supported me. They often got into fights when other teams went after my back."

At school, sports crept into everything Cammi did. She often used hockey, her favorite sport, as a topic for assignments. When the recess bell rang, she raced out the door, the first to choose up teams with the boys. Cammi admitted that she was "nonstop." "I was a bit of a klutz—spilling drinks or tripping. But when I played sports I was really coordinated. I played anything as long as I was active," she said.

Time-out

By Cammi's second year in high school, the boys had grown too big and strong. Although Cammi hit 5 feet 7 inches and more than 130 pounds, she was getting pretty banged up from the boys targeting her during games. She still wanted to play hockey, but Downers Grove North High School didn't have a girls' hockey team. About the same time, Cammi also discovered that she now enjoyed other activities with girls, such as dancing and putting on makeup. She longed to fit in socially—not just with sports. So, she put hockey on the back burner and joined high school basketball and soccer teams.

Even though she left the hockey team, Cammi continued practicing to perfect her game. At age sixteen, she was invited to play at the Assabet Valley girls' hockey camp in Massachusetts. Here she met coach John Marchetti, who also headed the highly respected women's hockey team at Providence College. After seeing her stickhandling, Marchetti urged Cammi to apply for a Providence scholarship.

"My brother Tony really set the standard for getting college scholarships for hockey. Then Robby and Donny followed," Cammi remembered. "In the back of my mind was the thought that I could get a scholarship, too. If I stopped playing hockey for two years in high school because the boys were too big, I could still play later."

Olympic Fever

In 1988, Tony went to the Olympics on the United States hockey team. The entire Granato family traveled to Calgary to cheer for him. Cammi delighted in the experience. "I decided that I wanted to become an elite athlete and experience the magic, too," Cammi said.

A year after the Calgary Olympics, Cammi entered Providence College. For the first time, she played hockey with females. Women's hockey turned out to be easy for her compared with the rough male games. But college-level sports proved a whole new experience. Suddenly, Cammi went from practicing two to three times a week with weekend games, as in high school, to being on the ice every day. She loved the challenge.

During Cammi's freshman year at Providence, USA Hockey, the main professional hockey group, announced tryouts for the U.S. Women's National Team. The team was to hold demonstration games only, meaning they were not part of Stanley Cup competitions. For Cammi, however, the formation of a national team gave her hope that she could some day play hockey after college. She eagerly hopped a plane to Colorado for tryouts.

Cammi skates her heart out during the final game with Canada at the 1998 Olympics.

The selection process involved a week of skating, hustling in games, and showing off skills for the judges. Although she made the team, Cammi had never worked so hard or been so tired. For the first time, she was competing with world-class athletes. Cammi realized how much she needed to perfect her game. Back at Providence, she launched into a fitness program to strengthen her body and mind. She lifted weights and rode a bike regularly in addition to team training. Slowly, she learned to eat a healthy, balanced diet, a difficult job for any college student.

After one year with Cammi, Coach Marchetti knew he had a winner. In her first season, Cammi broke Eastern College Athletic Conference (ECAC) records for the number of goals scored. "Cammi made Rookie of the Year her first year at Providence," Marchetti said. "She was probably one of the best players in the conference. She had vision, goals, and success."

> *"Cammi made Rookie of the Year her first year at Providence . . . She was probably one of the best players in the conference. She had vision, goals, and success."*

A Balancing Act

Cammi's hockey successes continued, and so did the challenges. Each year, Cammi made the national team while staying with the Providence Lady Friars. Schoolwork and national games became tough to coordinate. During practice and playing seasons, Cammi left college for weeks at a time. She missed classes and exams, often taking tests after a long break in her studies. For Cammi, the exhausting juggling act was worth the trade off to play hockey.

By graduation, the normally quiet, easygoing athlete had proved a powerhouse on the ice. Cammi was lead scorer with the 1992 national team. Moreover, she earned the title of best forward and was selected for the all-tournament team. At Providence, Cammi broke records for the most goals and assists. Her scoring helped the Lady Friars win conference titles in 1992 and 1993. Cammi achieved ECAC Player of the Year each of her last three years. She led Providence to so many wins that one 1998 Olympic player stuck a Providence sticker to the bottom of her skate for good luck. And this person never went to Providence!

Off the ice, Cammi worked to be a strong force for teammates. She realized the positive influence a close team can be. As assistant coach and then co-coach at Providence, Cammi was becoming a role model. "The first couple years, we had a great team but not a close one. By my junior year, we had the same goals and worked hard together. That's when we won our championships both years."

Looking Ahead

After graduation in 1993, Cammi took a semester off from school to think about her future. The Olympic Committee had just declared women's hockey a full medal sport. She wanted to continue playing hockey and focus on her goal of making the team. Yet the sport had a limited future beyond the Olympics. Cammi wondered how she could support herself with hockey, as her brothers did. Tony now played hockey for the San Jose Sharks; Donny was a minor league coach for the Columbus, Ohio Chill; and Robby was assistant coach for the Chicago Freeze while working with their dad. Cammi still played for the U.S. Women's National Team. But what she earned barely covered her room, food, and travel expenses. Not a way to make a living.

The following semester, Cammi entered a graduate program in sports administration at Concordia College in Montreal. Concordia's hockey team offered her a chance to advance her skills for the Olympics. Meanwhile, she could acquire an education that would help her earn a living coaching or managing a sports team.

Cammi quickly became top scorer on the team, but she worked hard for the spot. Canadian players exhibited a more guarded style than Cammi had played back home. Her coaches, Les Lawton and Julie Healy, helped her to develop that side of her game. Although Cammi wasn't the fastest skater or strongest shooter, her passing and instinct for the game were uncanny.

Family First, Then Hockey

While at Concordia, Cammi learned something important about herself beyond hockey. During a National Hockey League (NHL) game, Tony received a hard check that hurled him headfirst into the rink sideboards. Doctors discovered that a blood clot had formed from the injury. Tony needed surgery to save his life. Cammi and the rest of her family flew to Los Angeles to be with her brother.

Tony's surgery was a success, and he soon returned to hockey. But the experience changed Cammi's outlook on life, her family, and hockey. For the first time, she thought about injuries. But remembering Tony's courage inspired Cammi to overcome her fears.

"Tony's injury was the hardest thing I ever went through," Cammi remembered. "The most important thing to me is my family, and to have my brother's life in jeopardy was very scary. Here is a game that has been our life and common bond, and it abruptly almost takes his life. His accident showed me how small hockey really is in the scale of things. I also learned that if he can come back from that, I can come back from anything. It taught me a lot about his perseverance and courage. He has always been a huge inspiration for me."

> *"Tony has always been a huge inspiration for me."*

Olympic Tryouts

In 1997, the Olympic Committee held open tryouts for the games in Nagano, Japan. By then, Cammi was in her sixth year with the U.S. Women's National Team. A year earlier, she had been named Outstanding Forward at the 1996 Pacific Women's Hockey Championship and received the 1996 USA Hockey Women's Players of the Year Award. Nevertheless, Cammi knew competition was tough. She never let her playing guard down. The stakes were too high.

After initial tryouts, Cammi and 53 other selected athletes were invited to the USA Hockey Women's National Festival in Lake Placid. Here, the women played their hearts out in 24 games over five days. Five judges watched for speed, passing, and scoring in the matches. They agonized over their choices. For a player like Cammi, who was nearly out of college, this might have been the last chance at international team play.

At the end of the festival, Olympic head coach Ben Smith announced the 20 players for the first Olympic women's hockey team. Cammi's heart

"To hear my name called was such a relief . . . it was like someone handed me a key to devote my life to hockey, and maybe my dream will come true . . . to play in the Olympics."

pounded at the news. She not only made the team but was selected as team captain. As she told the *Boston Globe*, "To hear my name called was such a relief . . . it was like someone handed me a key to devote my life to hockey, and maybe my dream will come true . . . to play in the Olympics."

Training for the Olympics was a big commitment, taking fitness to a whole new level for Cammi. Before the season began, she lifted weights, ran, sprinted, biked, and skated on the ice twice a week. She put herself through a demanding schedule. Eight months before the Olympics, she prepared with teammates on and off the ice.

For the second time in her hockey career, Cammi worried about injuries. This time, she knew she would be heartbroken if anything interfered with her Olympic goal. The summer before the Olympics the worst did happen. She hurt herself badly, dislocating a disk in her back. Cammi couldn't even pick up a bag of groceries.

The slow healing process discouraged her. "It took more discipline than being an athlete," Cammi recalled. "I couldn't have intense training. I had to adjust and be patient and positive."

Bringing Home the Gold

Cammi's back healed in enough time for her to fulfill her dream. The entire Granato family minus Don, who had to coach, traveled to the Olympics for the second time. On February 8, 1998, the U.S. Women's

Olympic Hockey Team played their opening game with China. Cammi scored the first goal and went on to score again in the third quarter. She fired two of the four goals, wiping out China from the first round with a U.S. win of 4–0.

The game before the finals proved the most exciting for Cammi. "We were down 4–1 in the third period with ten minutes to go. We were playing a team we had never beat in national competition. A lot of teams would have packed it in and got negative, but we didn't panic. We just played our best game and scored six goals in eight minutes, beating Canada 7–4." With less than 40 seconds left in the first period, Cammi sparked the U.S. comeback by scoring. She went on to blast Canada with another powerful goal and an assist, earning three of the seven points.

With the gold in sight, Cammi went wild. What if they won? Could she really win a gold medal after all those years of dreaming? She found it difficult to wait for the last game to start.

After the United States beat Canada again 3–1, she was overwhelmed. "Winning was the most amazing feeling I've ever had," Cammi told CBS SportsLine Chat. "It's the culmination of everything I've worked for. Ever since I was very young I've dreamed of jumping around and walking away with a gold medal."

> *"Winning was the most amazing feeling I've ever had."*

Bringing home the gold turned Cammi's life upside down. Suddenly women hockey players were in demand. Cammi and her teammates whisked from one event to another. They met President Clinton at the White House, appeared on popular talk shows, and posed for a Wheaties cereal box. The greatest honor for Cammi, however, happened on April 19, 1998, Cammi Granato Day in Downers Grove, Illinois. Almost 7,000 neighbors showed up to cheer their hometown hero. Cammi felt proud to have represented her community at the Olympics.

Fame brought other rewards as well. Cammi received offers to endorse Nike products. She and her family made an AT&T commercial. Cammi began to feel that her dream of earning a living through hockey might come true.

Sharing the Dream

Throughout Olympic training and games, Cammi understood what a powerful role model she was for young girls, the role model she never had. That's why she scheduled her first appearances after Nagano at Downers Grove schools. She answered questions about getting hurt, how she trained, and whether she had her own teeth. She let the kids hold her gold medal. She told them that girls had another option now. They now knew 20 women on the Olympic team who play hockey, so they could, too.

Then Cammi worked with her mother to set up the Golden Dreams Foundation for children. The group raises funds and donates to groups that benefit children in need. "With salaries rising for athletes, these people are getting untouchable for kids," Cammi said. "I always said that if I got in that position, I would give back. Now is my time to give back."

After a few months, the Olympic craziness died down. Cammi forced herself to refocus. She went back to Concordia to complete her graduate diploma. Then, in the fall of 1998, she joined the Los Angeles Kings' new radio station, KRLA. With this job, Cammi became the only female broadcaster currently with the NHL and the second in the league's history.

The job gave Cammi the freedom to think about what tomorrow could bring—another Olympics, more seasons on the national team, serious talk about a women's hockey league, and more work in media and with her foundation. For the first time, the ground-breaking talented player looked forward to a future of endless hockey possibilities.

CAMMI'S OTHER INTERESTS:

Golf, boating, hanging out with nieces and nephews, seeing movies with her boyfriend, collecting sports memorabilia and sometimes Beanie Babies.

CAMMI'S HOCKEY TIP:

Have fun and work hard. Learn from other people around you. Most important, believe in yourself. You can do a lot if you are confident and focus your mind.

Chapter Four

Manon Rheaume

The most popular women's hockey player anywhere is Canadian-born Manon Rheaume. She broke gender barriers in two countries, the United States and Canada. At a time when few girls or women were allowed to play, Manon stood up to some of the toughest male players. In 1991, she goaltended with Quebec's celebrated all-male Trois-Rivierè's Draveurs. By age twenty, she made hockey history in an NHL preseason game. Then she signed with the all-male Atlanta Knights, another first. Manon's historic triumphs brought hope to other American girls who dreamed of one day earning a living playing the game they love.

Starting Young

Manon was born February 24, 1972. She spent her childhood in the quiet mountain town of Lac Beauport in French-speaking Canada. Here is where *her* hockey dreams began.

Manon came from an outdoor sports family. Pierre, her father and a contractor, constructed the family's house himself. Manon lived here with her father; mother, Nicole; and brothers Martin (two years older) and Pascal (eighteen months younger).

Like many Canadian fathers, Pierre built the house for winter athletes. A long wall lined with hooks held snowsuits, hockey skates, and ski poles. The basement doubled as an indoor hockey rink, and a large backyard skating rink attracted scores of neighborhood kids.

By age three, Manon had joined her older brother on the ice. At first, she wore the little white skates that girls used for figure skating. Her parents never imagined that their daughter would want anything else. But Manon preferred playing hockey with her black-skated brothers. She eagerly stood goal while they passed and shot pucks. For the next two years, Manon never tired of being a human goalpost. These early rounds at the net triggered a five year old's visions of playing hockey with the big boys in Quebec's Peewee Tournament.

Manon's father coached a team for her brothers. Usually, Manon tagged along to watch. Since the team was young, Pierre focused practices on skills, such as skating and stickhandling, instead of games. Within a short time, the boys improved enough to enter a tournament. There was one problem. No one had learned to cover the net.

Manon begged for the chance to goaltend. She had watched lots of practices. She knew the boys. She loved tending goal. She never let up on her father and mother. Finally, Pierre agreed. So did Nicole, who believed that no one should be kept from playing a sport. Her parents' only rule was that Manon put her goaltender mask on before she entered the rink.

"I guess they didn't want everyone to know I was a girl too soon," Manon wrote in her autobiography. "They didn't want to have to deal with the remarks.

> *"I guess they didn't want everyone to know I was a girl too soon . . . They wanted me to be judged on my performance, not on the fact that I was a girl."*

They wanted me to be judged on my performance, not on the fact that I was a girl."

Manon played an uneventful game. But the short time in front of the net proved something. No more figure skating. Hockey was for her. She would work to be the best goaltender she could be. Manon asked her father to file the tips off her figure skate blades. That way, she wouldn't trip while playing hockey.

"Manon has an unusually strong character and an enormous sense of pride," wrote her father. "When she decides on something, it has to happen."

Battles On and Off the Ice

Manon's decision to play hockey opened the flood-gates to years of battles, angry parents, and rules designed to sideline girls. Hockey is like a religion in Canada. Parents of even the youngest players take their kid's games very seriously. More than once

Manon heard, "There's no way that little brat is going to steal *my* son's place on a team." As with other athletic girls, Manon constantly had to prove herself on the ice.

For the next three years, Manon played hockey with Atom-age boys in the Northern League. Sometimes, she was too young or not good enough to goaltend for games. Then she played defense. This position helped to develop her backwards skating, stickhandling, and checking. But her heart belonged to tending goal.

The following year, Manon reclaimed the goal position. To keep it, however, she needed to improve. Her brothers went to different hockey camps to perfect their skills. She wanted to go, too. But the men at camp registration were sure she was a mistake. They told her that ringette, a form of hockey played only by girls, was down the hall. Manon never discouraged easily. She stuck to her story that she belonged, and she joined the other kids. She had won this first battle on her own.

Her next battle came when her father's assistant coach wanted to replace her with a new goaltender. She protested that she won her place fairly, but her father proved wiser. He knew that the other boy needed to play. There must be no doubt that a girl performed better. In the end, the boy lost the game. Manon's teammates grumbled that they wanted their goalie back. They wanted her. Manon believed she learned an important lesson from that game: "By facing a problem you solve it."

Hockey Rules

The Rheaumes' family life seemed to revolve around hockey. With three children playing, there was always a game. Relatives who wanted to see them traveled to one rink or another.

Although Manon did the same things as most kids, her main focus was hockey. She went to Lac Beauport Elementary School, liked school, and always earned great grades. Sometimes, she played baseball or other

> *"Manon has an unusually strong character and an enormous sense of pride."*

sports. She went skiing with the family and dressed her dolls when by herself. Yet, after a few minutes of doing something else, Manon always went back to hockey. She played "coach," with her brothers as pretend goalies. She played "hockey training camp." If her brothers wouldn't play, she invented imaginary hockey friends.

Over the next three years, Manon moved up the ranks of boys' hockey. During games, she received a lion's share of cuts and bruises. But Manon never complained. She credits her bravery on the ice to a comment her father once made. She had come to him with tears in her eyes after receiving some hard hits. Instead of comforting his daughter, Pierre said, "Macrame isn't painful. Choose!" Manon always remembered his words. She never cried because of a game again.

Proving Herself Another Time

Manon was thrilled to turn eleven. Finally, she was old enough to try out for her dream team with the Quebec International Peewee Tournament. Manon worked as hard as she could during training. Yet, she got cut from the top level AA league down to the CC group. According to her father, the coach hated that she was better than the other goalies. Moreover, he believed she couldn't handle the pressure. He had said, "There's no way a girl is going to play on my team."

Manon was disappointed—but not for long. She still had made the Peewee league, a dream come true. "They may think they're going to stop

> *"Someday they'll give in. They'll see that I am good."*

me, but I've wanted to play . . . for as long as I can remember, and I will. Someday they'll give in. They'll see that I am good."

The CC team worked well together. They worked so well that they represented their region at the 1983–84 world championship, a big deal in youth hockey. This championship consisted of 103 teams, including those from the United States, Switzerland, France, and Finland.

Manon rotated with another goalie for three games. Each time she blocked a puck, the crowd went wild. Cameras flashed. Everyone cheered for the only girl goalie. Manon wished they would cheer because of her goaltending instead of her being a girl, but she loved it anyway. The team made it to the semifinals before being eliminated.

Manon attracted attention from the minute the team names were posted. After the tournament, local reporters fluttered around Manon. They thought she was cute, an oddity. Besides, she was news. One headline blared: "Manon Goes to Peewee Tournament, the First Girl in 25 Years." *Le Progres Dimanche* published an article that quoted Manon saying, "One day, a woman will make the National Hockey League. If no one prevents her." She always aimed two steps ahead of herself—and the hockey world.

Time-out

In 1986, Manon moved into the next level of play. For two years, she tended goal for the boys' Bantam AA team. Now pressure closed in from all sides. Parents repeatedly voiced their dislike for a girl who wasted a place that a future NHL player could fill. Reporters continued to stay on Manon's tail. Worse yet, coaches and parents told opposing players to aim high for Manon's face. If bad manners didn't work, they wanted to scare her out. By the end of the second year, the coach felt the pressure, too. Manon spent much of her time on the bench.

Getting into the next Midget AAA league seemed out of the question. The barriers against girls playing hockey were too strong. Still, Manon played her heart out at the Midget AAA training camp. One coach seemed impressed with her style and reflexes. In the end, he backed off. Manon wound up in Midget AA, a step down.

As always, Manon tried to make the best of the team. But her teammates at this level were more into partying than hockey. Manon grew more and more discouraged. The week she turned seventeen, she quit hockey.

For the first time, Manon found time for something besides school and hockey practice. In her last year at Charlesbourg High School, she discovered boys and dating. After graduation, she completed a humanities degree from Sainte Foy Junior College near Quebec City. Manon looked forward to college and a communications degree. But something was missing for her: hockey.

Manon knew that playing with men was out, but she had heard of a women's team in Sherbrooke. At tryouts, she noticed the team's fairly high level of play. She also heard about hopes for the new world championships. Even more exciting, there was talk of making women's hockey an Olympic sport. These events sparked Manon's interest in hockey again.

"To get the best out of myself, I have to have goals to shoot for," Manon wrote. "The more pressure, the better I perform. Finally, I had found a new goal to pursue: the Olympics!"

The Road to the NHL

Manon traveled two-and-a-half hours once a week to play in Sherbrooke. Some games ran until two in the morning because women received leftover ice time. For late-night games, her mother accompanied her, since she didn't want her daughter traveling alone then.

In 1991, Manon's team earned the top spot in the province. Sherbrooke went on to place second in the Canadian championships in Montreal. Manon received a special trophy for best goaltender of the national series. She was proud to earn the award but longed for more ice time.

Manon and teammates at the 1998 Olympics.

By then, her brother Pascal was making his way toward the NHL. A scout for the Trois-Rivière's Draveurs, who had been watching Manon, too, invited both to training camp. Pascal easily made the Draveurs, a team similar to college level. Manon joined their second-string Louiseville Jaguars. She would also be backup goalie for the Draveurs. Although these positions were a step down, Manon was thrilled. She was the first girl to reach such a high level.

On November 26, 1991, one of the Draveurs' goalies became injured. During the middle of the second period, Coach Drapeau sent in Manon. The team was losing 5–1. Manon played 17 minutes against the Granby Bisons. After stopping 13 of 16 shots, a puck smashed into her mask. The shot split her left eyebrow, which bled enough to block her vision. The coach pulled her from the game to get stitches. Manon never received another chance with that team. She returned to the Jaguars, who rarely won a game. Still, the hockey world started to take the bright-eyed woman player seriously.

"It takes quite a personality to stand in front of the net when you know everyone is watching and judging you," Coach Drapeau admitted. "If the young guys . . . even had half as much character as she did, more of them would make it to the NHL."

> **"If the young guys . . . even had half as much character as she did, more of them would make it to the NHL."**

49

Now Manon was the hottest sports news around. The media circus that would shadow Manon the rest of her career began in earnest. Every Quebec radio and television station interviewed her. Reporters from all over North America called. *Playboy* magazine even offered $40,000 for an interview and a nude photo. Manon flatly turned down the offer.

"Money can't replace personal pride," she wrote.

The magazine offer hit a nerve with Tampa Bay manager Phil Esposito. Why not invite the popular female hockey player to training camp? She could get a chance at the NHL. Meanwhile, she could stir up some interest in the team. Manon jumped at the chance.

Training with the Big Boys

Manon kept up with the guys for the two weeks of camp. She handled her share of sit-ups and push-ups. She stopped all 15 shots during her first practice game. As far as most other rookies were concerned, this twenty-year-old earned the right to be at camp. Only everyone expected more from Manon because she was the first girl at NHL camp.

"Throughout training camp, I had to do inter-views, photo sessions, television and radio shows, and return dozens of phone calls while the other players were playing golf, having fun, and taking it easy," Manon wrote. "There was no choice for me but to think, live, and breathe hockey 24 hours a day."

At the end of camp, Tampa Bay played an exhibition game with another NHL team, the Saint Louis Blues. Esposito gave Manon her big chance to goaltend the first period. She played 20 minutes, blocking seven of nine shots. Even though Tampa lost 4–6, the media went wild. Reporters called from around the world. Then Manon appeared on the David Letterman show. Her popularity soared in the United States as well as in Canada. A 1992 Quebec survey of favorite athletes listed her fourth. That same year, the newspaper *USA Today* ranked her thirteenth. *Time* magazine called her the seventh wonder of the sports world.

Mixed Reviews

Reactions to Manon's groundbreaking game varied. Some believed that the attention was good for women's hockey overall. Others feared that playing with boys was the only way girls could get recognition. They worried that if too many females aimed to play with guys, girls' and women's teams would suffer.

The fanfare was just what Esposito wanted. Besides, he liked the playing he saw in training. Manon wasn't Tampa Bay material yet, but she had promise. Therefore, Tampa Bay offered her a three-year contract to train with their farm club, the Atlanta Knights of the International Hockey League (IHL). At training camp, Manon would play every day and develop her skills and her body. If she improved,

Manon would play third-string goalie for the Knights. Perhaps, one day she could rejoin Tampa Bay.

Manon knew that her NHL chances were limited. She was only 5 feet 7 inches and 130 pounds, compared with 6-foot goalies who were 200 pounds. At most, 25 juniors out of the 250 ever make a NHL team. Still, Manon loved the idea of being part of minor league hockey. For three years, she could get paid to live her hockey dream—no matter where it took her.

Far from Home

Manon moved into an apartment in Atlanta. At first, she found speaking English a problem. She had to think hard about every word that was said. Sometimes, her head ached by the end of the day just from listening. After a while, speaking English became easier. Still, Manon preferred hanging out with French-speaking players. It was just simpler.

In addition, French reminded Manon of home. Atlanta was too far away to fly home every weekend. She met few women at work and had little time to find friends. She had had a boyfriend who was also a major league hockey hopeful. But that ended. Manon's brother was no longer on a nearby team, as in Quebec. He now trained with the New Jersey Devils. Each night Manon went home to an empty apartment.

"There's always lots to do—hockey cards to sign, letters to answer, and phone calls to return—but sometimes talking to my stuffed animals isn't enough," she wrote.

For most Knights games, Manon warmed the bench. On December 13, 1992, Coach Gene Ubriaco sent her into the second period of a game against the Salt Lake Golden Eagles. Manon faced four shots, allowing one to slip past her, before she was pulled. Again, she made history. At age twenty, Manon became the first female to compete in a regular season professional hockey game.

> " . . .sometimes talking to my stuffed animals isn't enough."

On to the Olympics

The following March, Manon played in the first World Women's Hockey Championship with the Canadian national team. Here is where she really shined. She posted a three-game win, with two of them shutouts. Manon earned the tournament's most valuable player honor. Moreover, she gained the respect of female hockey players everywhere.

Between 1992 and 1997, Manon played for six all-male minor league teams. Her first win came during the opening game of the 1993–94 season. Manon started goal with the Knoxville Cherokees of the Eastern Conference Hockey League. She stopped 32 of 38 shots fired by the Johnston Chiefs, helping her team win 9–6. The win lifted a big weight off her shoulders.

> **"I was under a lot of pressure from the media . . . Getting the first win took away some of that pressure."**

"I was under a lot of pressure from the media," Manon said. "They expected me to perform. Getting the first win took away some of that pressure."

Each team that Manon played for reaped a gold mine worth of publicity after adding her to their roster. A reporter from the *Ottawa Sun* (April 26, 1996) called Manon "the hottest marketing name in hockey." Manon now earned more than $250,000 (U.S.) a year through endorsements alone. Toyota, Starter sports clothes, and Reebok shoes were a few of the companies who paid her to use their products. Singer/movie director Barbra Streisand bought the movie rights to her autobiography *Manon: Alone in Front of the Net.*

Besides playing second-string with the guys, Manon continued as first-line goalie with Canada's national women's team. Her outstanding goaltending at international games helped the team bring home the gold every time. During the 1994 world championships in Lake Placid, New York, Manon recorded three wins and no losses. Following the games, she was named to the All-Tournament team, another honor. At the 1996 Pacific Rim Tournament in

Richmond, British Columbia, Manon only gave up one goal in three games.

Off-season she guarded the goal for different teams of the Roller Hockey International League. First, Manon went with the New Jersey Rock'n Rollers, then the Ottawa Loggers, and later the Sacramento River Rats. Again, she was the only female on these teams. Manon told *Sports Illustrated for Kids* (September 1995): "The roller hockey puck is light, and the shots are fast. It's good for improving my reflexes."

The media hounds continued to dog her. There were Manon trading cards, colored posters, and oodles of articles. Not all stories put Manon in a good light. Some were downright nasty. Many people still refused to accept a girl in boys' or men's ice hockey, let alone the minor leagues. Others doubted Manon's skills.

"The worst is reading things about me that aren't true," Manon said. "It's hard to deal with media that always tries to find something wrong with you."

Olympic Silver

Manon and two other goalies competed for two spots on the 1997 national team. The winning goalies would compete in the world championships in Kitchener. After four days at training camp, Manon was cut.

According to coach Shannon Miller, "We have three goaltenders who, without question, can start and play in net. . . . Rheaume has been good and she

55

has been great but not consistent. The other two at this point in time for this event play more consistent hockey for us."

The news was a major setback for Manon. Still, she vowed to return in top form for Olympic tryouts. Despite her fame, Manon knew she had to prove herself to make the Olympic team. "I especially was disappointed because 1997 was my best pro year," Manon explained. "I knew it (not making the team) was because of the different timing between men's and women's hockey. So I just came back for the Olympic team and did what was needed to make it."

The following September, Manon returned to Olympic camp for five months of training. "We didn't make the team until December," Manon recalled. "We had to deal with pressure every single day because we wanted it so badly. At the same time, we prepared the team for the Olympics. They started cutting players after a few months. I wanted to be happy for what happened to me, but it's hard to lose a friend on the way."

Manon and Lesley Reddon rotated the two goal spots on the Olympic team. Manon started the opening Nagano game with Finland, which Canada won 4–2. During the second round, Canada beat Sweden 5–3. Then, Canada lost the gold to the United States by 3–1. Even with the loss, Manon realized she had been part of a historic event once again.

"The Olympics was one of the greatest moments I ever had," she said. "I want to go back to the next one."

Manon lines up with the Canadian team before the final 1998 Olympics game with the United States.

The Future

In the summer of 1998, Manon, now twenty-six, married national inline hockey player and former minor leaguer Gerry St. Cyr. That August, she announced they were having a baby. For the time being, Manon put her hockey career on hold. She and Gerry continued to teach hockey and organize tournaments for children and adults. Manon missed the entire 1998–99 season. After Dylan was born in May, she started workouts again. Manon wanted to continue with the national team and have another shot at the Olympics. Who knows? Maybe she would return to professional hockey.

Few critics doubt that Manon is a serious hockey player. She serves as a real star in a game that has captured a continent. Her highly visible career has played a key role in the growth of women's hockey. Through Manon, girls can see that anyone with talent and a strong will—male or female—can play professional hockey and achieve SPORT SUCCESS.

MANON'S OTHER INTERESTS:
Her growing family; shopping; cooking; crafts, such as pottery, to decorate the family home.

MANON'S HOCKEY TIP:
Be positive in what you do. It's harder for girls because we are not supposed to be playing this sport. Believe in yourself and never quit.

Chapter Five

Erin Whitten

Erin Whitten has her share of wins and awards as star U.S. goaltender. But what makes Erin stand out among goalies everywhere is her awesome list of women's hockey firsts. She was the first U.S. woman to play professional (pro) hockey and the first woman ever to play a complete game in the pros. Moreover, she became the first woman to win a pro game. That means, besides women's college and national teams, Erin has played with the big boys—and won!

Early Wins

Erin was born on October 26, 1971 in Glens Falls, a small town in northern New York State. The same town became home to a training rink for the Adirondack Red Wings, Detroit's minor league team that feeds into the National Hockey League (NHL). As a young girl, Erin attended Red Wings practice games with her father, Peter Whitten, and followed NHL games on television.

Not surprisingly, one of Erin's first hockey memories was of the men's U.S. Olympics team. The men had just won the gold in 1980, and Erin's dad was listening to the final game on the radio. At the time, Erin was eight years old and already into the hockey team spirit.

"I remember listening to the Olympic game against the Soviet Union from outside the house," Erin said. "I was playing in the snow and hearing all the excitement after the U.S. team won. I started pretending I was on the team and screaming, 'We won! We won!' I did my impression of goaltender Jim Craig, dancing around with the U.S. flag wrapped around me."

"We won! We won!"

That same year, Erin tried out for the local hockey league. By then, she had been skating about four years. "It was the kind of thing I started with the boys in the neighborhood. I was so interested in sports and such a tomboy when I was little, I just wanted to play hockey, too. My dad got behind me and taught me how to skate. I remember being on the ice when I was four and skating along on my double-edge skates—and freezing."

Erin started playing ice hockey at the local rink when she was six. In warm weather, she and the neighborhood boys slipped into roller skates and shot pucks around the street. When they were old enough for the ice hockey league, Erin signed up with the boys.

Erin's first tryout would have ended most people's hockey career. But she was gutsy even then. "I had skates that were two sizes too small," she recalled. "My feet hurt so much. I just cried and pushed myself to skate with the others. The coach tried to help me, but I kept saying that I could do it—not just now. I was the last skater back to the line."

Erin earned a reputation early on as the kind of player who never gave up. "Erin's mother and I attribute some of her determination to a problem she had at birth," said her father. "At six weeks, Erin was hospitalized with a rare stomach disorder and needed surgery to save her life. She survived and thrived. But we feel that having to fight to stay alive had an effect on her character. Now, once she makes up her mind to do something, she does it."

Erin did make the house league, the team everyone gets shuffled into when not on the traveling team. She played goalie and forward, the only girl on the team. The next year, however, she made the traveling team, still the only girl. "I was going on trips with all these boys. I had a baseball cap like the rest of the guys and long blonde hair."

A Family Affair

All the while Erin had the support of her warm, caring family. Her mother, Joan Whitten, and father drove her to countless practices, tournaments, and at least 25 games a year. Erin's older sister, Kelly, tagged along in all kinds of weather to games up to 200 miles (320 kilometers) away. Erin's father, who also ran a community health center, coached her teams.

"We had ungodly early morning practices," her father recalled. "When the Red Wings were in town and taking up ice time, we had to be willing to be on the ice at any hour. For 5:30 AM. practices, we got up at 4:30 A.M. It took me a half-hour just to shove Erin's hair under her helmet. The league was concerned that her long, blonde hair would catch on something during the game. We also didn't want her to be a target for the boys."

Erin rarely had problems with other kids on the ice. She worked hard and proved that a girl could skate and stop the puck. "There were always one or two kids out to get the girl. Occasionally, someone said they thought I shouldn't be there," Erin added. "But I fought through that and said I have just as much right to be here as you do."

At Kensington Elementary School, Erin played whatever sports she could, particularly hard driving ones. She joined in street hockey, football, and sometimes soccer—anything the boys let her play. The same was true at home.

"I never played what girls were interested in," Erin said. "My friend Ashli and I tortured our Barbies because we didn't like them. We played hide-and-go-seek, kick the can, and ghost in the graveyard. We made up a game where we would throw the ball into the air. Everybody would tackle whoever caught the ball. That game got pretty rough."

> *"I loved . . . how the goalie was the center of attention—the one who makes or breaks the games."*

Erin played forward until age ten. Then, her interest turned to goalie. "My dad and I were attending Red Wings practices pretty often, and my eyes kept being drawn to the goalie," Erin explained. "I loved the equipment and how the goalie was the center of attention—the one who makes or breaks the games. I decided I wanted that kind of pressure on me."

Erin asked to play goal part time. The other time, she stayed a forward. This went on for a couple years. By age twelve, Erin was sure she wanted to switch to goaltender full time, a decision she has never regretted.

Erin stayed on the traveling team until the end of sixth grade. Then she left Glens Falls Junior High School for Mountainside Christian School, where her younger sister Lisa goes now. For the next three-and-a-half years, she attended private school. At first, she was happy there, but Mountainside had no athletics. Slowly, Erin began to miss her neighborhood friends—and hockey.

Breaking Traditions

Erin transferred to Glens Falls High School in the middle of tenth grade, a bad time to be a new kid on the block. Hockey season was in full swing, and everybody had established social cliques. Erin found it difficult to fit into her new school. She was determined that the second year would be different. It would be a hockey year, even though the high school only had a boys' team.

Before Erin could try out, however, she had to pass a series of tests. "The big fear is a girl getting hurt," coach Don Miller explained. "In New York State, when a girl wants to play a boys' sport—or the reverse—there are special endurance tests to make sure she has enough strength for the boys' team. A panel of people, including her physical education teacher and her doctor, must attest to her physical ability. Erin's tests were done by the athletic director, so I wouldn't be biased."

Erin wondered why she was the only athlete to take these tests. Still, she took them and passed. Then, she tried out for the hockey team and made it—a first for Glens Falls and New York high school hockey.

The local media went crazy. Television stations showed up at practice to broadcast the girl who played the rough game of hockey. Reporters greeted Erin whenever she played. Suddenly, she went from somebody who was an unknown to someone everybody knew as the girl on the boys' hockey team.

Breaking into Boys' Hockey

To teammates who had played with Erin before, however, she was just another goalie who could stop pucks. On the road, it was different.

"At one school, spectators threw tampons on the ice," Coach Miller remembered. "Erin's reaction was to skate out, scoop them up, and throw them in the net without making a big deal. Another time, people shouted some pretty nasty catcalls. I never saw her react in a negative way. She played the game, never looking affected, and they stopped. Maybe it made her stronger."

That first year, Erin rotated with two other goalies. She never started as goalie, even though everyone wanted to see the girl play. Erin worked hard on team drills and improved quickly. Off-season, she played softball and field hockey. Equally important, Erin earned good grades and made lasting friends.

Meanwhile, Coach Miller learned more about including a girl on his team. On bus trips, he let Erin ask another girl to join her. At night, she sat in the front of the bus. At other rinks, Miller asked for a place where Erin could dress. Usually, she changed in a closet. Between periods, the coach allowed her into the locker room to feel like part of the team.

"Erin is a very stable and even-tempered person," Coach Miller said. "Other people would not have been too happy with some of the situations she experienced. Yet, Erin never complained and

> **"Erin never complained and always seemed prepared."**

always seemed prepared. She wasn't trying to prove anything by playing on a boys' team. She just liked to play the game."

By senior year, Coach Miller was starting Erin in key games. "One of Erin's most exciting games was against Albany Academy, a prestigious prep school. The two teams were evenly matched, but Albany always seemed to have the edge before. That day, we were down. Erin went in as goal, and she was phenomenal. She won the crowd over, and we won."

Erin became the first female hockey player to participate in a New York high school state championship. Glens Falls didn't win, but Erin felt good knowing that she had helped her team make it to the championships. The same year, she earned the

1988–89 all-conference honorable mention for her outstanding ability to stop the puck. She had posted a 21-win, 9-loss, 2-tie record by blocking 84.9 percent of the shots against her—a great record for a boy or girl.

"To be a goalie, you have to be pretty courageous," Coach Miller explained. "You have people coming at you at great speeds who will do anything to put the puck in the net. Therefore, you have to be good with your hands, and you have to be strong enough to move the heavy equipment around. Erin knew what was going to happen before it happened. She prepared for her moves. She was always calculating. That's how she beat you."

College Hockey

Erin used the same purposeful thinking to choose a college. She wanted a good education in a small-town school that would give her a scholarship for women's hockey. The fall of 1989, Erin enrolled at the University of New Hampshire (UNH), a school of about 10,000 students. This was her first chance to play hockey with women.

"I had to adjust to a women's game," Erin said. "The pace was slower, and there were fewer big hits coming at me than from the boys. Still, it was cool to be in the same locker room and have the team around you on and off the ice."

The New Hampshire team won championships during Erin's first two years. "I never won a championship before. What I remember most is being part of a team and having similar experiences and so much fun. The second two years, we lost to Providence College. Cammi Granato was the main reason for the losses."

Besides hockey, Erin took classes in government, thinking she would like to be a lawyer. Soon she discovered that she disliked the courses she needed to make law a career. In her junior year, Erin switched to psychology, the study of why people behave the way they do. She liked the information, and psychology applied to many different careers. Still, Erin remained undecided about what to do after college. Playing men's professional hockey lurked in the back of her mind. For now, however, she enjoyed being in a sorority and focusing on her favorite sport—hockey.

By senior year, Erin's goaltending dominated the Eastern College Athletic Conference (ECAC). She earned ECAC goalie-of-the-year each for her four years and player-of-the-week twice. She set school records for the most saves in one game (46), a record that still stands today. She also topped school charts for the most saves in a season (501) and the most saves in a college career (1,540). Her college save percentage reached an amazing 91 percent.

Going National

Erin played so well that she qualified for the U.S. Women's National Hockey Team in her junior year. "I could have tried out for the 1990 team, but I didn't think of women's hockey at the time. I loved the men's game," she recalled. "After the U.S. team took the silver in Ottawa, I reconsidered and decided to try out in 1992. Once on the team, I realized what an honor it is to play for your country. I thought: Wow, I'm representing the United States!"

Erin soon discovered the struggles of juggling college and the national team schedule. Sometimes, she missed weeks of school at a time. She took homework with her on the road and scrambled to catch up after returning to school. Luckily, her professors were willing to work with her. "The spring of 1992 wasn't an easy semester, but it was worth it," Erin said. "What I learned was to always talk with your teachers."

Dreams Come True

Erin graduated from the University of New Hampshire in 1993 and landed a job as a hockey instructor in Glens Falls. At the rink, she met other instructors who competed in the National Hockey League. A few had seen Erin play and coaxed her to try out for the pros. As Erin told *Child Life* Magazine, "At first I was unsure, but I knew I'd regret it if I didn't give it a shot."

In the fall of 1993, Erin competed in her first professional tryout. After some tough training sessions, she made the Adirondack Red Wings. Erin was thrilled to make the team that first spurred her interest in hockey as a child.

Reactions came swiftly to a female invading the male stronghold of pro hockey. Much of the interest mirrored the days when Erin played high school hockey. An avalanche of television cameras and reporters swooped onto the rink for practices and games. Some wondered if the team's choice was a publicity stunt. Erin was the second goaltender on a men's team. Before her, Manon Rheaume had broken the male hockey barrier by goaltending for Tampa Bay in an NHL exhibition game. Although Manon never played another NHL game, her game created considerable fanfare for Tampa Bay.

"I tried not to pay attention to all the hype," Erin said. "I was doing what I always dreamed of—playing on a professional hockey team! It was so incredible, the speed of the game and the competition. I loved it all. I just stayed focused on my job stopping pucks."

"I was doing what I always dreamed of—playing on a professional hockey team!"

Being Part of the NHL

Much of the season, Erin sat on the bench. Her first big chance to play came in the second period of an exhibition game. "I let in two shots," Erin recalled. "But I had the most amazing glove save I ever had."

Erin moved onto the East Coast League's Toledo Storm. During the second period of a game against the Dayton Bombers, she went in to replace injured Alain Harvey. The tough twenty-two year old continued to block the puck for the last two periods, stopping 15 of 19 shots and helping the Toledo Storm score a 6–5 win. Erin became the first woman to win a game in men's professional hockey.

Erin blocks China's shot during the 1997 World Games.

For three years, Erin continued to play on men's teams. After Toledo let her go, Erin joined the Dallas Freeze. Off-season, she played professional roller hockey with the Pittsburgh Phantoms. Erin believed that playing year-round sharpened her reflexes and kept her in shape.

On each team, Erin discovered one or two men who were unhappy with a woman as goalie. "If I got hit in the mask, teammates expected me to stay down, get out of the net, and off the ice," she said. Erin determined to work even harder to earn their respect.

Often she faced great danger to prove how tough she was. During one Dallas game, a shot knocked off her helmet. The helmet rolled out of her reach, leaving her totally unprotected. Erin's teammates grew frantic as the play continued. Instead of calling for a time-out, however, Erin hung in there until the whistle blew.

If Erin felt fearful or uneasy playing with men, she never let on. Erin told *The New York Times*, "Playing against men you're at the bottom rung of the ladder, and you scrape to get playing time and respect. There's a lot of satisfaction when you gain that respect."

Yet, those three years proved a great challenge. Erin was often on her own, dressing separately and always being followed by reporters. Moreover, she was constantly being judged. Many hockey fans never got over the fact that she was a woman intruding in a man's world. "Yet, I never once heard a word of complaint," her father recalled.

A Hockey Slump

Erin continued to play on the U.S. National Team while goaltending for the pros. Then, the Olympic Committee announced that women could participate in 1998. The national team, and Erin, began to train together more seriously. Anyone who wanted to try out dropped everything and arrived in Dedham, Massachusetts. Here, team hopefuls trained five hours every day, including daily morning practice followed by gym exercise, weight training, and running. After the workout, the women held team meetings and played games. Erin was one of three goaltenders competing for two positions on the Olympic team. Coaches watched their every move in practice and exhibition games.

During the entire pre-Olympic tour, Erin went into a slump. In the Three Nations tournament, she carried the team to a 6–2 victory over Finland by stopping ten shots. But she had hoped for a shutout to further prove her skills at stopping the puck. The next game with Canada continued the downward spiral.

"We were winning 4–1," Erin explained. "Then came their pressure shots. They ended up winning with very little time left."

When the coaches announced the team choices soon after the tournament, Erin was left out. She never showed her disappointment. Still, not making the team was a blow. She had played hockey all her life and started as goal for almost every game until the Olympics. To be excluded now seemed unfair.

Erin keeps her eye on the puck, always prepared to block a goal.

"I've always been disgusted about the outcome of the 1998 Olympics for Erin," Coach Miller emphasized. "She carried the team before the Olympics as goaltender. Perseverance is her thing. They stole the dream from her."

The Road Ahead

Erin decided she needed a change. She left training and took time off from hockey. "I just played to have fun," Erin said. "It helped me get back into the game without jumping into serious events where all the pressure is on me for a win or loss."

Erin also took time to think about what was important to her. She continued to run camps for teaching children to play hockey. She married her hometown honey, Tim Hamlen, and started a new job at a rink in Exeter, New Hampshire. And she began training for the next Olympics. "I'm going to try out for the next Olympic team," Erin said in a determined voice.

In 1999, Erin got her chance to shine with the national team again. She tended goal for two games of the Women's World Championship in Finland. Both games were shutouts, with Erin never letting a single goal get past her. The U.S. team won the gold, and Erin earned the third highest save percentage (94.4 percent) of the 12 goalies who played.

"There is life after disappointment," her father emphasized.

Now, Erin's sights on the next Olympic team seem more real than ever. She has an amazing list of firsts behind her. And she has the opportunity to make one of women's hockey's first major comebacks. With Erin's courage and talent, who can doubt that this gutsy goalie will help the United States bring home the gold the second time around?

ERIN'S OTHER INTERESTS:

Work out in the gym; shop; watch movies; spend time with new husband, Tim Hamlen, and family.

ERIN'S HOCKEY TIP:

Do whatever makes you happy. Never give up. If you say something is too hard and never try, you are missing out on a big part of life.

Chapter Six

Hayley Wickenheiser

The world is used to seeing fifteen-year-old Olympic skaters and gymnasts. But most observers like their hockey players, well—full grown. Forwards, especially, need the strength and sharp mind to plow through advancing opponents, smack the puck, and score a goal.

That's where Hayley Wickenheiser comes in. In 1994, the fifteen-year-old Canadian forward became the youngest—some say the best—national hockey player in the world, male or female. Even hockey great Wayne Gretzky took two more years before entering professional hockey at age seventeen. What is more amazing is how Hayley knew she would play world-class hockey at a time when no national women's teams existed.

First Skates

"Hayley loved hockey from day one, and she went for it," remembered her mother, Marilyn Wickenheiser.

Marilyn first introduced her daughter to skating as a toddler. She bundled Hayley onto a sled and pulled her around the public rink while she skated. Sometimes, the two watched Hayley's father, Tom Wickenheiser, play hockey. To Marilyn's surprise, Hayley always cried when they left the rink early. Hayley wanted to watch until the end. She wanted to skate herself.

Marilyn and Tom were both teachers in the small town of Shaunavon, Canada. Hockey was always big in Canada, especially in towns of five hundred people, but only for boys. Still, Hayley's parents believed in all sports for personal growth and supported their daughter's interests. Tom, a physical education teacher, put Hayley in skates at age three. He flooded the family's large backyard for a neighborhood rink. When Hayley was four, he bought her her own skates. By age five, Hayley played organized hockey on a boys' team, with her father as coach. Not long after, she was determined to make the NHL.

"We didn't want to dissuade her," Marilyn said. "We encouraged her to look at other sports, too. She was always a natural at any sport."

For the next seven years, Hayley played hockey with boys in Canada's minor league. In addition, she figure skated. "I had figure skating class with hockey practice right after," Hayley explained. "I wasn't serious about figure skating, but I continued three times a week for about three or four years. For me, figure skating was another way to get on the ice."

Hockey Came First

Hayley grew up well rounded, interested in just about everything. At Shaunavon Elementary School, she liked learning and being creative. She took art classes for a few years and began piano lessons at age seven, which lasted for seven years.

But Hayley's first love seemed to be sports. Besides hockey, she played softball and volleyball.

She joined other kids for lunchtime soccer and football. "I was usually the only girl, but the boys let me play," Hayley added.

Despite these varied interests, Hayley refused to give up hockey. She spent every spare minute on the family's homemade ice rink. During frosty Canadian winters, she would glide over the ice, wind whipping against her face. One evening about midnight, her father awoke to swishes and thuds coming from the backyard. He checked out back and discovered his nine-year-old daughter skating. She soared up and back under the glow of a garage light, firing pucks into a net.

"Hayley was always motivated and highly disciplined," Marilyn recalled. "She was a good student and excels at whatever she tries. Her younger brother Ross and sister Jane work hard and do their best, but Hayley seems driven. She is always determined to have her way.

"For example, when Hayley was about six, she was in trouble for something. The next thing I know she took a brown paper bag and put some things in it. She told me she would go out and left walking toward her best friend's house down the street. I called ahead on a hunch she would run away there. When the mother told her they didn't have room, Hayley just played for a few hours outside. After dinner, she came home as if nothing happened."

Hockey Dreams

Hayley's father coached teams she was on until she was twelve. For the first five years, he assigned her to defense rather than up front on offense. Tom worried that his daughter was in too big of a rush. He wanted her to think like a hockey player. He wanted to teach her patience.

"As a child I was very intense," Hayley admitted. "I was busy and active. I couldn't sit still."

At about age ten, her dad switched her to center. He knew that the skills his daughter had learned on defense plus her skating speed and fierce, powerful game would make his daughter a great forward. Hayley's father served as more than her teacher and coach on the team. He dealt with anyone who didn't want a girl around ice hockey, and the numbers were great. Most of the time, he took the angry comments. Hayley was left to play the game.

"It was easier for me being a female because he was there," Hayley remembered. "I guess it wasn't always easy, though. Dealing with parents was the worst part. I can remember one parent following me off the ice. She said I shouldn't be on the ice and should leave her son alone. It was a competitive game, and we were both the best players on our teams."

> **"I guess it wasn't always easy."**

Sometimes, boys came after Hayley and made comments. The attacks got worse after she became a center. Once boys targeted her as the girl, she received more than her share of hits and cuts. Still, Hayley never cried or tattled. Instead, the tough, fast skater clobbered the other team by scoring goals. Hayley earned the most valuable player (MVP) award almost every year she played minor hockey.

In the back of their minds, Hayley's parents always hoped she would give up the idea of hockey fame. Her dad told CNN, "There was a time, I forget exactly how old Hayley was, when I sat her down. I tried to explain life. She was a good athlete in all sports—softball, volleyball, basketball. I told her these were sports with an up side. She probably should concentrate on them. Hockey, I said, really didn't have a future. Hayley said she didn't care. She wanted to play hockey."

Hayley's World Changes

Then two things happened that changed Hayley's hockey future and the Wickenheiser household forever. The first involved a worldwide women's competition. In 1990, when Hayley was twelve, the International Ice Hockey Federation launched the first Women's World Championship in Ottawa, Canada. The final game between the United States and Canada blared from the Wickenheiser television. Hayley stayed glued to the screen.

She found some things about the game weird. She thought that Team Canada's girlie pink jerseys with white pants looked strange for such a strong sport. So did the pink flags and banners decorating the arena and *zamboni*, the machine that cleans the ice. She wondered why everything wasn't in Canada's red and white national colors.

But there was so much more to delight her—the excited crowds, the wonderful female players. Hayley had never known any women hockey players as role models. Good female players were always compared to boys or men. Now, she saw women with the same speed and toughness as men, despite their ugly uniforms. Finally, women's hockey created the same frenzy and respect as the men's game. Hayley could hope for a future in hockey—with the national team.

The second event of 1990 involved Marilyn and Tom's new teaching jobs in Calgary. The entire family moved. Suddenly, Hayley's chances to play hockey in the future soared. Calgary was home to the Canada Winter Games and the Olympic Oval. The Winter Games were Canada's answer to Olympics for kids. Each yearly event had the same format as the international Olympics. There were opening and closing ceremonies and games in between.

Leagues of kids from each province competed after team tryouts before the games. Star players were encouraged through hockey camps and special training classes. The Oval was the center that provided training for youth and adult hockey programs, including the Olympic and national women's hockey teams. Those kids who continued to excel moved onto Canadian Olympic teams, although women's hockey was just an Olympic dream in 1990.

Before the move, Hayley was in the process of trying out for the Canada Winter Games on the Saskatchewan team. Once in Calgary, however, she wound up playing for the province of Alberta. By then, she was twelve years old and barely five feet tall. During the games, she played against girls of sixteen and seventeen. Hayley proved that age and size had nothing on strong stickhandling and quick skating. Again, she was voted most valuable player. This time, it was for an outstanding job with the 1991 gold medal 17-and-under team.

"We thought Hayley enjoyed the sport and learned life lessons from it. We never dreamed it would go anywhere," Hayley's mother said. "Then she became involved with the Canada Winter Games. We learned she had potential. We knew the national team was in Calgary. There was some place to go with hockey."

Adjusting to a New Home

The move proved scary for Hayley her first year. Life was easier in Shaunavon. She knew everyone. She could walk everywhere. Calgary was a big city. Hayley found making friends difficult at St. Vincent DePaul Junior High.

Sports helped Hayley feel more comfortable and meet people. Besides the Winter Games, she played basketball and volleyball in grades seven, eight, and nine. All three of those years, she won athlete of the year.

During grades eight and nine, the school basketball team won city championships. Hayley played point guard. "I remember the final game for city championship in ninth grade," Hayley said. "The match was a two-point difference game that came down to the last basket. We were in our own gym, and everyone was cheering. We had an exciting finish and won. I scored about thirty points in the game and was pleased just to be part of the team that won."

Throughout junior high, Hayley continued to play hockey regularly. She played defense again because the club team needed her in that position. In Canada, local clubs, rather than schools, sponsored youth hockey teams. Then, as now, anybody could play. When kids got older, they tried out with kids from other areas. Clubs could be pretty important for kids who wanted to be hockey players as adults. The club system provided the base for Winter Games and national teams.

With more options in Calgary, Hayley was able to join a girls' team for the first time. "Playing with girls was different," Hayley remembered. "I really enjoyed the social part of it. I liked changing in the same dressing room instead of a separate room or boiler room. The girls' team was a way for me to make friends, since I really didn't know anyone."

Hayley noticed one problem with the girls' team. The caliber of play wasn't challenging enough. To keep her skills sharp, she needed to step up her game.

After a year on the girls' team, Hayley went back to playing with boys. The switch proved tougher than expected. At fourteen years, Hayley had to try out, and the quality of big city play was high. Even worse, a lot of people wanted to discourage her from trying out for the team because she was a girl.

Hayley made the AA hockey team. Once on the team, the mood around her never turned more welcoming. Hayley kept getting too many extra hits on the ice. Some boy from another team was always smacking into her after the whistle blew. "I loved the game, so I kept playing," Hayley said.

The Road to Nationals

Hayley went to Bishop Carroll High School for grades ten through twelve. Students here studied mainly on their own. Teachers were there if students needed them, and there were some seminars but no actual classes. "The school was good for me. I was self-motivated and enjoyed that type of atmosphere," Hayley said.

In tenth grade, she played basketball and volleyball as well as boys' AA bantam hockey with the Northwest Bruins. The next year, Hayley decided to try out for the national team. From then on, her life changed rapidly.

"My parents wanted me to play with the Canada Winter Games a second time instead," she said. "They thought I was too young for a national team. But I really wanted to try out."

By age fifteen, Hayley had shot up. She added muscle and height and improved her game. Hayley easily made the national team, a dream come true. She became the youngest player ever on the national team.

"Everyone nicknamed me High Chair Hayley because I was so young," Hayley admitted. "When we were on the ice, however, there was no age difference. Everyone was equal. I think I earned my way on the team."

"I think I earned my way on the team."

Once Hayley made the national team, she left the boys' team and returned to playing forward. Her schedule became busier with national training and

Hayley proved she was a powerhouse during a 1997 World Championship game with the United States.

schoolwork. In eleventh grade, Hayley dropped high school basketball. By her senior year, hockey was her only sport.

"The kind of high school I went to suited my training schedule," Hayley said. "I could work on my own and work ahead when I would travel. Sometimes, the workload was difficult. I had to be disciplined, but it was possible. I gave up a lot of social life to work. But I really loved hockey and had no problem with it."

In 1994, Hayley went to the world championships in Lake Placid, New York, with the national team. "I had one of my worst injuries there," Hayley remembered. "I slid into the boards and tore ligaments in my ankle. I was out for the round robin games but was able to play the final and semifinal tournament games." Hayley wound up with one assist in three games, and Canada won the gold medal.

Over the next few years, Hayley helped Canada win gold medal teams at the 1995 and 1996 Pacific Rim games and the 1996 Three-Nations Cup. By the 1997 World Championships at Kitchener, Ontario, she had developed her famous rough-and-tumble game. The 5-foot, 7-inch forward scored four goals with five assists in five games, a good showing. Although not usually the highest scorer, Hayley's play always overpowered the game.

As Team Canada defense Judy Diduck told *Time*, "If Hayley can't get around you, she'll go through you."

The Surprising Silver Medal

The Canadian national team displayed an amazing worldwide winning streak. Hayley wanted to help continue Canada's success at the 1998 Olympics. But first, she had to try out and make the team.

In the fall of 1997, the Oval invited 30 of Canada's best female hockey players to Calgary. Hayley, who was in her first year at the University of Calgary, put aside her studies in sports medicine. For six months, she trained together with the other women athletes. After the first three months, coaches chose the team of 20 women who would finish training and go to the Olympics. Hayley remembered being chosen as one of her happiest hockey moments. Still, the news felt bittersweet.

"The hardest part was being happy for yourself but sad for teammates who didn't make it," Hayley recalled.

"The hardest part was being happy for yourself but sad for teammates who didn't make it."

Besides training, some women Olympic athletes visited schools. Hayley represented ice hockey to hundreds of children. Everyone was eager to hear about the sport and upcoming Olympics. Hayley enjoyed encouraging young athletes, especially the girls. She began to feel like the role model she had never had.

As the Olympics grew closer, the team spent all their time together. Once at the Olympic village, coach Shannon Miller tried to keep the women focused. Still, the atmosphere at Nagano was electric for Hayley. Although her sister and brother stayed home, her parents were there cheering for her. She met athletes from around the world in the Olympic village. Most exciting was seeing the same stars she had watched on television as a child.

To help the athletes feel at home, parents were asked to fill boxes with special mementos. Each hockey-playing daughter received a package a day. Hayley looked forward to the poems her mother tucked into every package.

"The day they played the final game with the Americans, we enclosed a plastic dish," Marilyn said. "Part of Hayley's card said to 'dish it out to the Americans.' "

That's exactly what Hayley had intended to do. She had been playing her usual bulldozer style, and the Canadians were favored to win the gold. Then, things started going wrong. During the game against Sweden, Hayley fractured her elbow. There were also rumors about a strained knee. Neither injury was enough to stop Hayley's game.

"I had an injection to freeze the elbow," Hayley said. "It didn't bother me that much. I don't think it bothered my game." Although she played a good game, onlookers reported that Hayley never seemed to put any power behind her shots. In the end,

Canada earned the silver medal, losing the gold to the United States. Even though Hayley felt terrible, she still greeted fans and signed autographs.

"At first, I was really disappointed," Hayley recalled. "As I look back, however, just being at the Olympics and representing women's hockey was pretty exciting."

After the Olympics

The few months after the Olympics, Hayley made a whirlwind round of school visits and public appearances. The Easton equipment company asked her to become their spokesperson, which added visits to corporation mettings. Hayley also accepted an invitation to practice at the Philadelphia Flyers rookie summer camp. She saw the camp as a way to improve her game. Flyers manager Bob Clark thought Hayley's gutsy playing fit the Flyers style. He told one reporter that Hayley "kind of plays like forward John LeClair, only a little meaner."

Flyers camp was exhausting. There were exercises, skating drills, scrimmages, and pumping iron every day for two weeks. Media dogged the girl player in a boys' camp. The demanding schedule was more than Hayley had expected. But she kept up with the rookies and earned their respect by the end of training. They even threw Hayley into the pool to celebrate, a rookie tradition.

Look to the Future

After summer camp and Olympic madness, Hayley took some time off to rest. She camped in the Alberta mountains and mountain biked. And she got back into another sport favorite—softball.

By fall, Hayley returned to juggling her college studies and women's hockey. Hayley made the 1998 national under-22 women's hockey team. Now the team trained for the Christmas Cup Tournament. At the tournament, Canada beat Germany and Switzerland. The Canadians were back in step, hoping to build another winning streak before the next Olympics. Hayley continued as top player in the tournament.

According to Wally Kozak, Olympic Oval's senior coach, "Hayley is one of the most dynamic and explosive players in the world. She is fiercely competitive and immensely talented. She is extremely fast and powerful on skates and has one of the hardest shots in women's hockey. On our team, she plays all positions. She takes charge and makes things happen."

The Christmas Cup was Hayley's first experience as captain, a big job for someone nineteen. Yet, she proved to be the ideal captain.

"She adjusted her ability to relax and stay calm when needed, and she led by example," Kozak continued. "She has leadership qualities on and off the ice that make her a special player. She is a very total package in what she

"She takes charge and makes things happen."

brings to a team—competitive and always giving her best. With guidance and coaching, she is maturing with her gifts."

For Hayley, the hockey future looks bright. Still, the nineteen-year-old leaves her options open about what lies ahead. At school, she studies medicine in case professional hockey never develops. She also takes business courses, which would help with a possible hockey career. Besides ice hockey, she plans to try out for the national Olympic fastball team, perhaps placing her on two Olympic teams at once. She is talented in so many areas and so many hockey positions that Canadian officials call her "the Franchise."

College roommate and Team Canada defense Judy Diduck summed up Hayley's successes for *Time*: "She's accomplished a lot but still is young, relatively speaking. Maybe in four years another prodigy will come along, and we won't have to say she plays like Gretzky but that she plays like Hayley Wickenheiser."

HAYLEY'S OTHER INTERESTS:

Playing piano and listening to music, learning to play guitar, camping and other outdoor activities, school, reading, and learning.

HAYLEY'S HOCKEY TIP:

Practice on your own—skate, shoot pucks, and play a lot to practice your skills, so playing becomes easier.

Hockey Talk
Glossary

body checking using the hip or shoulder to slow or stop an opponent who has control of the puck.

center the team position in the zone closest to the opposite net that helps a player score. The center has the job of *facing off* to gain control of the puck at the beginning of each play period.

defense the team position that protects the zone closest to their team's net from the opposite team moving in and scoring.

defensive zone the area of the ice rink closest to a team's net.

face-off the action that begins game play. The referee drops the puck between the sticks of two opposing centers, and they scramble to gain control.

forward the team position closest to the opponent's net.

goal the point received after hitting the puck into the opposite team's net.

goaltender (goalie) the player who guards their team's goal net, stopping the puck from entering the net.

league a group of sports teams that compete among themselves.

offense the team position that moves ahead and scores.

offensive zone the area of the ice rink closest to the opponent's net.

puck a flat, round, hard rubber object that glides on the ice rather than bouncing like a ball.

referee a game judge who scores goals and calls time, penalties, and other game plays.

varsity the highest level team that represents a school or college.

zamboni the machine that cleans the ice.

Hockey Connections
Where to Find More Information

General Sports for Girls and Women

National Association for Girls and Women in Sports
1900 Association Drive
Reston, Virginia 20191-1599
703-476-3452
www.aahperd.org/nagws.html

In 1999 NAGWS had its 100th birthday. The group's been fighting to promote females in sports since 1899. Members helped pass Title IX and battled for respect for women's programs. One of its major public awareness efforts includes National Girls and Women in Sports Day, February 4th. Be sure to celebrate the day by playing your favorite sport!

Women's Sports Foundation
Eisenhower Park
East Meadow, New York 11554
(800) 227-3988
(516) 542-4700
www.lifetimetv.com/wosport/index.htm

This group works toward increasing opportunities, grants, and recognition for girls and women in sports. Tennis star Billie Jean King founded WSF in 1974 to support gender equality and to encourage and recognize females who play sports through its International Women's Sports Hall of

Fame, which has inducted 94 women since it was founded in 1980. Contact them for education guides, videos, general sport's information, and their list of awards and scholarships.

Girls Incorporated
120 Wall Street
New York, New York 10005-3902
(212) 509-2000
www.girlsinc.org

This group runs programs to help girls become stronger, smarter, and bolder. They have three sports-related programs as ways for girls to learn about teamwork and risk taking. Contact them for information about a given sport and starting programs in your area.

U.S. Olympic Committee
1 Olympic Plaza
Colorado Springs, Colorado 80909
(719) 632-5551
www.olympic.usa.org

They have the scoop about the Olympics, Olympic camps, and how to get involved.

Big Ten Conference
1500 West Higgins Road
Park Ridge, Illinois 60068-6300
(847) 696-1010
www.bigten.org

This association coordinates girls' and boys' sports at 11 Big Ten universities. One of its special programs for younger girls is Dream Big. With this information and activity program, the Big Ten hopes to encourage more girls in grades K–8 to enjoy sports. They offer a free kit for helping young girls and coaches start programs for different sports and to keep them going.

Girl Scouts of USA
420 Fifth Avenue
New York, New York 10018
(212) 852-8000
misc@gsusa.org

Girls Scouts has a new national program called GirlSports. This program hopes to increase opportunities for girls to try new sports. What they really want is to see girls have so much fun that exercise becomes a lifelong habit, and a healthy one, too. Besides offering materials to girls ages five to seventeen, they hold sport leadership and national summer sport events. They also sponsor health and fitness activities. Contact them for sports posters, coloring books, and diaries.

YWCA of the USA
726 Broadway
5th Floor
New York, New York 10003
(212) 614-2858

The 135-year-old group seeks to empower females through its network of 400 YWCAs in 4,000 communities. Each YWCA offers fitness and sport programs for females of all ages. This pioneer organization for girls and women is the only group to hold a seat on the U.S. Olympic Committee.

National Organization for Women (NOW)
1000 16th Street, NW, Suite 700
Washington, DC 20036
(202) 331-0066
www.now.org

This national organization focuses on issues of equality for females. It usually has little to do with sports. But NOW will represent anyone in court who feels unfairly excluded from playing a sport because of being a girl.

Hockey Groups for Girls and Women

USA Hockey
1775 Bob Johnson Drive
Colorado Springs, Colorado 80906-4090
(719) 576-USAH (8724)
usah@usahockey.org

This group is the governing body for hockey in the United States. It organizes and trains men's and women's teams for international tournaments and the Olympics. It also oversees rules and coordinates amateur teams for all-age players—girls and boys.

Canadian Hockey Association
1600 James Naismuth Drive
Gloucester, Ontario K1B 5NA
www.canadianhockey.ca/dev.wom

This is Canada's answer to USA Hockey. The group sponsors hockey clubs for all age players across the country. These include the national women's team and programs for kids, international tournaments, world championships, and Olympic games. Canadian Hockey also links players, coaches, and volunteers involved in local hockey groups across Canada.

Staying Hot
Further Reading

Ayers, Tom. *The Illustrated Rules of Ice Hockey*. Nashville, TN: Ideals Children's Books, 1995. Great explanation of the game, including players, rules, and equipment for girls and boys.

Johnson, Anne Janette. *Great Women in Sports*. Detroit: Visible Ink Press, 1996. Good collection of women in various sports, including Manon Rheaume.

McFarlane, Brian. *Hockey for Kids*. New York: Morrow Junior Books, 1996. Overview of hockey for young readers.

——. *Proud Past, Bright Future: One Hundred Years of Canadian Women's Hockey*. Canada: Stoddart, 1994. Interesting history of hockey that emphasizes Canadian women's hockey from its beginnings to the present.

Rheaume, Manon and Gilbert, Chantal. *Manon: Alone in Front of the Net*. Toronto, Canada: HarperCollins, 1993.

Bibliography

Books

Allen, Kevin. *USA Hockey*. Chicago: Triumph Books, 1997.

Etue, Elizabeth and Williams, Megan. *On the Edge: Women Making Hockey History*. Toronto, Canada: Second Story Press, 1996.

Fischler, Shirley and Fischler, Stan. *Everybody's Hockey Book*. New York: Charles Scribner's Sons, 1983.

Harari, P. J. and Ominsky, Dave. *Ice Hockey Made Simple: A Spectator's Guide*. Los Angeles, CA: First Base Sports, Inc., 1996.

Johnson, Anne Janette. *Great Women in Sports*. Detroit: Visible Ink Press, 1996.

McFarlane, Brian. *Hockey for Kids*. New York: Morrow Junior Books, 1996.

——. *Proud Past, Bright Future: One Hundred Years of Canadian Women's Hockey*. Canada: Stoddart, 1994.

Smith, Lissa, ed. *Nike is a Goddess*. New York: Atlantic Monthly Press, 1998.

Wolfe, Bernie. *How to Watch Ice Hockey*. Bethesda, MD: Full Court Press, 1985.

Web Sites

Information about Women's Hockey
http://www.cs.toronto.edu/~andria/

U.S. Whips Finland 6-2/Cammi Granato Hired as Color
Commentator—plus other articles about various hockey
women
http://www.canoe.ca/HockeyWomen.html

Erin Whitten—A Gutsy and Talented Athlete
http://www.govnews.org/mhonart/gov/us/fed/
congress/record/extensions/_msg00353.html

Women in Sports
http://www.makeithappen/com/wis/icehock/whittene.htm

USA Today latest news
http://www.usatoday.com/olympics/owg98/owgih/
owgihw.htm

Roller Hockey International
http://www.oro.net/~rhiglo/RHI/pr/Clinic

Allo, Manon!
http://loggers.ottawa.com/News/sun_manon.htm

Sports Illustrated Womensport: The New Pioneers
http://cnnsi.com/features/1997/womenman/
nprheaume.html

Women's Goalies Friends and Rivals/Devastated Hockey
Women Feel Empty in Loss to U.S.
http://www.thestar.com/editorial/olympics98/
hockey/980207SPT03_OLY-Goalies7.html

Manon Rheaume's Official Sacramento River Rats Home Page
http://www.riverratshockey.com/manon1.htm

CBS Sportsline Chat—Gold Medalist Cammi Granato/ Meeting the Press by Hayley Wickenheiser
http://web7.sportsline.com/u/chat/htm

Women's Hockey Takes Center Stage
http://www.sj-sharks.com/sharks/thegame/ womens_hockey.html

Lifetime Online—Breaking through Women's Hockey
http://www.lifetimetv.com/sports/breaking_through/ players.html

U.S. Women Beat Canada to Even Series 6-6
http://espnet.sportzone.com/olympics 98/news.html

Making History Is Goal for First Women's Team
http://www.orlandosentinel.comsports/olympics/ stories/whock0206.htm

Articles

Associated Press. "Survey: Fewer Girl Athletes Get Pregnant." *Chicago Tribune*, 11 July 1998.

"Extra! Extra! Women's Soccer to be Played at the 1996 Olympics." *Sports Illustrated for Kids*, January 1994, v. 6, n. 1, p. 14(1).

Freeman, Miller. "Females of the Future." *Sporting Goods Business*, September 1997, v. 30, n. 14, p. 24(1).

"Girls Active in Sports Do Better in Classroom." *New York Times*, 29 March 1997.

Hatch, Ruth. "Social Studies." *Canada's Globe and Mail*, 26 July 1993.

Lapointe, Joe. "U.S. Women First at Gold in Ice Thriller." *New York Times*, 18 February 1998.

Longman, Jere. "Women's Hockey: No Fights, Just Skating." *New York Times*, 7 April 1997.

Lopiano, Donna. "Her Say: Female Athletes Setting Examples, Records." *Chicago Tribune*, 4 February 1996, WN 6.

Martin, Tamara. "My Questions Are about a Female Hockey Goaltender." *Sports Illustrated for Kids*, August 1995, v. 7, n. 8, p. 20(1).

"Odds and Ends." *Wall Street Journal*, 4 January 1994.

Preston, Brian. "Shots on the Goal." *Saturday Night*, February 1995, v. 110, n. 1, p. 71 (3).

Skalko, Sherry. "Cammi Granato: Goal-Getter." *Sports Illustrated for Kids*, December 1996, v. 8, n. 12, p. 70(3).

Smith, Gwen. "The Home Team." *Maclean's*, 7 April 1997, v. 110, n. 14, p. 68(2).

Whitten, Erin and Cameron, Layne. "Erin Whitten: The Puck Stops Here." *Child Life*, January-February 1995, v. 74, n. 1, p. 4.

Wojciechowski, Gene. "Title IX Comes of Age." *Chicago Tribune*, 4 August 1996.

Index